What Is a Sentence?

A **sentence** is a group of words that tell a complete thought. Every sentence begins with a capital letter and ends with an end mark.

sunny days

This is not a sentence. It does not tell a complete thought.

Picnics are fun on sunny days.

This is a sentence. It tells a complete thought.

Read each group of words. Write **yes** if the words make a sentence. Write **no** if the words do not make a sentence.

1. Let's go to the park.

2. Travel together.

3. I will make sandwiches.

4. You can bring juice.

5. Snacks at noon.

Draw a line from the words on the left to the words on the right to make sentences.

6. We had a great   under the trees.
7. We ate lunch   were there.
8. All my friends   day at the park.

Sentences Have Naming Parts

A **naming part** of a sentence tells who or what the sentence is about.

My family went on a trip.

My family tells who this sentence is about.

The trip took six hours.

The trip tells what this sentence is about.

Underline the naming part of each sentence.
Then circle **who** or **what**.

1. Our family visited Yellowstone Park.   who   what

2. The park has lakes and springs.   who   what

3. People camp in the park.   who   what

4. Stars fill the night sky.   who   what

5. Forests are everywhere.   who   what

6. Hikers climb hills.   who   what

Write a naming part to finish the sentences.

7. _____ is fun to visit.

8. _____ and I go there a lot.

Sentences Have Telling Parts

The **telling part** of a sentence tells what someone or something is or does.

Visitors **see wildlife**.
The animals **run freely**.
The park **is interesting**.

Which words tell what visitors do?
Which words tell what the animals do?
Which words tell what the park is?

Underline the telling part of each sentence.

1. Owls hunt at night.

2. Elk eat green plants.

3. Eagles nest in the park.

4. Water shoots up from underground.

5. Hikers walk down trails.

6. The forest is quiet.

Write a telling part to finish the sentences.

7. Campers _____.

8. A squirrel _____.

Word Order in Sentences

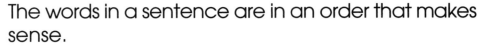

The words in a sentence are in an order that makes sense.

Jamal likes to walk on the beach.

These words are in order. They make sense.

walk likes Jamal to the beach on.

These words are not in the right order. They don't make sense.

Write each group of words in the order that makes sense.

1. plays Jamal the in sand.

2. likes He make to sand castles.

3. walks waves in the He.

4. finds seashells He.

5. are Some shells white.

6. Write a sentence. Check the word order.

Statements

A **statement** is a sentence that tells something. A statement begins with a capital letter and ends with a period (.).

I eat fruit every day.
Yogurt tastes good with fruit.

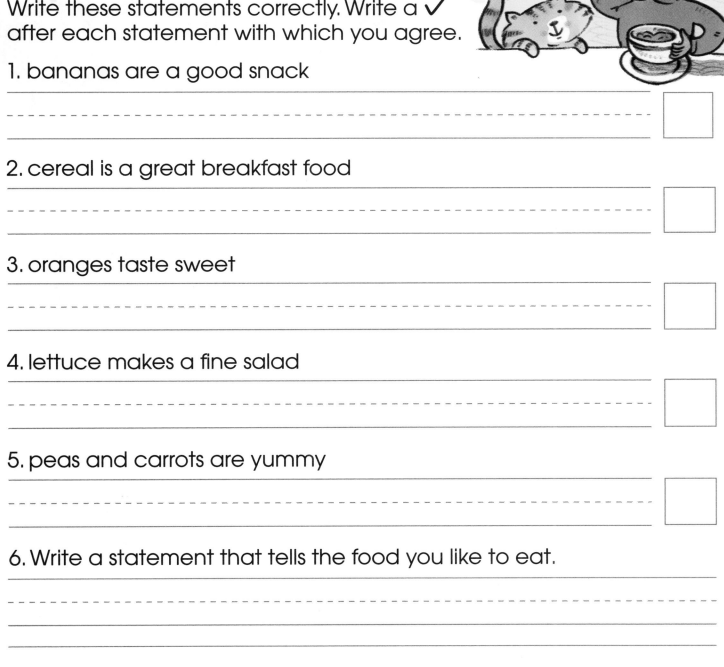

Write these statements correctly. Write a ✓ after each statement with which you agree.

1. bananas are a good snack

_____

2. cereal is a great breakfast food

_____

3. oranges taste sweet

_____

4. lettuce makes a fine salad

_____

5. peas and carrots are yummy

_____

6. Write a statement that tells the food you like to eat.

_____

Questions

A **question** is a sentence that asks something. A question begins with a capital letter and ends with a question mark (**?**).

What do you want for lunch?
Do you want tomato soup?

Write a period at the end of each statement.
Write a question mark at the end of each question.

1. Do you like pizza _____

2. I like pizza with mushrooms _____

3. I do not like pizza with sausage _____

4. What do you like on your pizza _____

5. Do you ever have pizza for dinner _____

6. Have you ever made your own pizza _____

7. Write a question about food.

_____

_____

_____

8. Write a statement that answers the question.

_____

_____

_____

Exclamations

An **exclamation** is a sentence that shows strong feeling. An exclamation begins with a capital letter and ends with an exclamation point (**!**).

I can't believe we won!
We're the best!

Write an exclamation point after the exclamations.
Write a period after the statements.

1. My team played our last soccer game today _____

2. The most amazing thing happened _____

3. The score was 3 to 3 _____

4. Our team got the ball _____

5. We made a goal _____

6. It was awesome _____

7. Three cheers for the champs _____

8. Write an exclamation.

Commands

A **command** is a sentence that tells someone to do something. A command begins with a capital letter and ends with a period.

Look at our team trophy.
Tell how you won the trophy.

Write these commands correctly.

1. pass the ball

2. run fast

3. don't use your hands

4. keep your eye on the ball

Write the correct end mark to finish each sentence.
Draw a line to the kind of sentence it is.

5. The game is over now_____   question

6. Who is the best team _____   exclamation

7. Hooray for the Roadrunners _____   command

8. Give them a trophy_____   statement

Write Directions

Directions tell how to do something step-by-step.

Read these directions.

How to Make an Ocean in a Bottle ◄-------- title

If you can't visit the ocean, you can make one in a bottle. Get a plastic soda bottle, blue food coloring, and mineral oil. } ◄-------- things you need

First fill the bottle 3/4 full with water. Next add a few drops of blue food coloring. You can add some tiny plastic fish or shells if you want. Then fill the bottle with mineral oil. Last, twist the cap on tightly. Hold the bottle sideways. Tip it back and forth. See the ocean waves! } ◄-------- steps

What do these directions tell?

How do you know what to do?

Underline the command words in the directions in red: **Get, fill, add, twist, Hold, Tip, See**. These words tell what to do. Underline the time order words in blue: **First, Next, Then, Last**. These words tell when to do it.

Plan Your Directions

What do you know how to do or make? Choose one idea to write about.

My directions will tell

_____

- -

_____

_____

- -

_____

Drawing is one way to plan what you will write. Draw each step. The first box could show what you need. The second box could show what you do first. Use as many boxes as you need.

1.	2.	3.
4.	5.	6.

Show your pictures to someone. Tell them about each step.

Do the steps make sense?   yes   no

Are the steps in the right order?   yes   no

Do you need to add a step to your plan?   yes   no

Draft Your Directions

Look at the pictures you drew. Now write the steps of the directions in order.

Use words such as **first**, **next**, **then**, and **last** to make the steps clear. Begin each step with a command word, such as **get**, **fill**, **add**, **put**, **cut**, **find**, **mix**, or **pour**.

Title: _____

Directions: _____

_____

_____

_____

_____

_____

_____

_____

_____

_____

_____

Check Your Directions

You can use **proofreader's marks** to help you correct your writing.

This mark ≡ shows where a capital letter should be. This mark ⊙ means add a period. This mark ℐ means take out.

Use proofreader's marks to correct this paragraph.

g̲e̲t a plastic bottle, blue food coloring, and mineral oil ⊙

~~What is your favorite soda?~~ First fill the bottle 3/4 full with water.

Water tastes good. next add a few drops of food coloring

Use proofreader's marks to fix the directions you wrote. Now check your directions.

Did you tell all the steps?   yes   no

Did you use time order words?   yes   no

Do all your sentences fit the subject?   yes   no

Did you begin sentences with capital letters?   yes   no

Did you put end marks at the end of the sentences?   yes   no

Publish Your Directions

Publish your writing to share it with others. Make a final copy of your writing.

Choose one way to share your writing.

- Read your directions with a family member.
- Give your directions to a friend to read and follow.

A **noun** is a naming word. Some nouns name people or animals.

My uncle lives on a farm.

The word **uncle** is a noun. **Uncle** names a person.

My uncle has a rooster.

The word **rooster** is a noun. **Rooster** names an animal.

Read the sentences. Underline the nouns. Then write each noun next to its picture.

1. My uncle has many cows.

2. See my cousin feed the pigs.

3. The hens and chicks are eating.

4. There is my aunt with her horse.

What Do Nouns Name?

Some nouns name places or things.
Take the cows to the barn.
The word **barn** is a noun. **Barn** names a place.
The truck is ready.
The word **truck** is a noun. **Truck** names a thing.

Read the story. Underline each noun.
Then write the nouns in the chart.

The family is busy working on the farm. The cows are being milked. Hens are laying eggs. A neighbor is painting the fence. The horse waits in the barn to be brushed. My uncle is out in the field on his tractor.

People	Animals	Places	Things

Write a sentence. Underline the nouns.

Nouns 15

Using **a** and **an**

The words **a** and **an** are **articles**. Articles are used before nouns.

Use **a** before a word that begins with a consonant.

   A hen sat on **a n**est.

Use **an** before a word that begins with a vowel or vowel sound.

   An ostrich laid **an e**gg.

Write **a** or **an** to complete the sentences.

1. If you give _____ elephant _____ peanut, she'll want peanut butter.

2. If you give _____ ant _____ crumb, he'll want a whole cake.

3. If you give _____ horse _____ apple, she'll want a bushel.

4. If you give _____ otter _____ fish, he'll want a seafood platter.

5. If you give _____ fox _____ egg, she'll want it scrambled.

One and More Than One

Some nouns name one.

Can a giraffe run faster than an elephant?

The nouns **giraffe** and **elephant** name one.

Some nouns name more than one.

Giraffes run faster than elephants.

Giraffes and **elephants** name more than one. Many nouns that name more than one end with **s**.

Write one of the nouns to complete each sentence correctly.

1. Some _____ run very fast.

   animal   animals

2. The _____ runs 70 miles an hour.

   cheetah   cheetahs

3. There are no _____ that run. They glide.

   snake   snakes

4. Tiny _____ move very slowly.

   snail   snails

5. A herd of _____ can travel fast.

   horse   horses

6. Can you run as fast as a _____ ?

   cat   cats

Singular and Plural

Nouns with es

Nouns that end with **s**, **x**, **ch**, or **sh** add **es** to name more than one.

glass ⟶ glasses　　bench ⟶ benches

fox ⟶ foxes　　bush ⟶ bushes

Finish each silly sentence. Choose words from the oval. Add **es** to make each word mean more than one.

box　fox
lunch　bunch
peach　beach

1. I see _____ in _____ .

2. I see _____ of _____ .

3. I see _____ on _____ .

If a noun ends with a consonant and **y**, change the **y** to **i** and then add **es**.

cherry　cherries

Write each noun to mean more than one.

4. strawberry _____

5. penny _____

6. story _____

Other Plural Nouns

Some nouns change into a new word to name more than one.

man ⟶ men
woman ⟶ women
child ⟶ children

Some nouns stay the same to show more than one.

one fish ⟶ two fish
one deer ⟶ two deer

CHILD

CHILDREN

FISH

Draw a line to match each noun that names one to the matching noun that means more than one.

1. tooth   sheep
2. foot   geese
3. sheep   teeth
4. goose   feet

men   sheep
women
children

Write the total and a word from the oval.

5. 4 girls + 6 boys = _____ _____

6. 8 mothers + 5 aunts = _____ _____

7. 5 black sheep + 14 white sheep = _____ _____

8. 10 fathers + 6 uncles = _____ _____

Special People and Animals

The special names of people and animals are proper nouns. All proper nouns begin with a capital letter.

> Aunt Alice has a dog.
> Her dog's name is Tootsie.

Aunt Alice and **Tootsie** are proper nouns.

Correct this story by writing this mark ≡ under each letter that should be a capital. Then write the capital letter above. The example shows you how.

Pet Parade

The neighborhood is having a pet parade. A̲unt alice and

tootsie are there. So is tom with ruff. Here come pat and matt

with their cats, fluff and muff. There is wayne with his pig,

petunia. See carmen's snake called slither. Last in line is

grandpa jones. He calls his silly goat whiskers.

Write a sentence about someone's pet.

_____

_____

_____

_____

Titles and Abbreviations

A **title** goes before a person's name. Titles begin with a capital letter. Most titles are followed by a period.

Mrs. Tittlemouse   Mr. Bank
Ms. Clover   Dr. Pulltooth
Miss Twinkle

An **abbreviation** is a short way of writing a word. You can use an abbreviation to write the name of a day, month, or place in an address. Abbreviations for states do not need a period.

Sun. ⟶ Sunday   Fri. ⟶ Friday
Mar. ⟶ March   Nov. ⟶ November
TX ⟶ Texas   MI ⟶ Michigan
Rd. ⟶ Road

Draw a line to match each word with its abbreviation.

1. Saturday   Ave.
2. Pennsylvania   Mar.
3. Avenue   Sat.
4. March   PA

Write an abbreviation for each word.

Come to Josh Morgan's BIRTHDAY PARTY.

When: 2:00 on _____ , _____ 13
              Saturday   March

Where: 7 York _____
              Avenue

Towanda, _____
         Pennsylvania

Special Places

Some proper nouns are names of special places.

Nouns	Proper Nouns
country	United States
state	Alaska
city	Fairbanks
street	Bell Lane
park	Yellowstone Park
forest	Pawnee Forest

Read the postcard. Find the name of each special place.
Write this mark ≡ under letters that should be capitals.
Write the capital letters above.

Dear Grandma,
   We are having so much fun in arizona. Today we went to red rock canyon. The rocks are so red. Tomorrow we drive to the tonto state forest. We will camp there. Love,
   Chris

Mrs. Mary Morgan
28805 flower street
roseville, michigan
        48805

The names of your street, city, and state are proper nouns.
Write your address.

Days, Months, and Holidays

Some proper nouns name days, months, and holidays.

Thanksgiving is the last Thursday in November.

May
Saturday
Windmill Day

Choose proper nouns from the oval to complete the sentences.

1. In the country of Holland, children have a

_____

holiday called _____ .

2. It is celebrated in _____ .

3. It is on the second _____ in the month.

Use this mark ≡ to show where to add capital letters in the story.

   I will spend july and august with my father. He lives in

denver, colorado. On independence day we will visit the

grand canyon. I will be away until labor day. That is the first

monday in september.

Write a sentence about your favorite holiday. Tell why you like it.

_____

_____

Book Titles

The name of a book is its title. The first and last words in a title begin with capital letters. Other important words in the title also begin with capital letters. When you write a book title, underline it.

Arthur's Halloween
Froggy Goes to School
Tales from the Jungle Book

Write these book titles correctly.

1. bird watch

_____

_____

2. the great kapok tree

_____

_____

3. if you give a pig a pancake

_____

_____

4. coyote dreams

_____

_____

5. the dinosaurs came back

_____

_____

Compound Words

Compound words are two words joined together to make a new word.

back + pack = backpack
rain + coat = raincoat
pop + corn = popcorn

Draw a line to match each pair of words to make a compound word.

1. foot   glasses
2. bare   foot
3. sun   prints
4. sea   shells

Write the compound words to finish this story.

Today I went to the beach. It is fun to take off my shoes and

_____

walk _____ . Look at everyone's

_____

_____ in the sand! I bought a new

_____

pair of _____ to shade my eyes.

_____

Before I went home I hunted for _____ .

I had a great day at the beach!

More Than One Meaning

Some words have more than one meaning.
The word **shoot** can mean a tiny plant.
The word **shoot** can also mean throw a basketball.

The words in the oval have more than one meaning.
Write one of these words to answer each riddle.

watch
step   cold
swing

1. I'm a sickness that makes you sneeze and cough.
   I'm also a chilly temperature.

   _____

   What am I? _____

2. I'm something that tells time.
   I'm also something you do with your eyes.

   _____

   What am I? _____

3. You can play on me at the playground.
   I'm also something you do with a bat.

   _____

   What am I? _____

4. I'm something you do with your feet.
   I'm also a part of a stairs.

   _____

   What am I? _____

Write a Poem

A **poem** is a special kind of writing that describes something or shows feelings. Many poems have short lines and few words. Some poems have rhyming words. Some poems follow a pattern and other poems do not.

Read this poem out loud.

> Rain
> Rain on the green grass.
> Rain on the tree.
> Rain on the swimming ducks,
> But no rain on me!

The words in this poem form a picture.

Little star
night.   shining
darkest   bright,
the up   light you

Here is a different kind of poem.

the subject	➤ My bird, Nicky
three describing words	➤ Soft, tiny, lively,
four-*ing* action words	➤ Chirping, singing, chattering, flying
three nouns	➤ Pet, buddy, friend,
the subject	➤ My bird, Nicky

1. Which poems have words that rhyme?

_____

_____

_____

2. Which poem follows a special word pattern?

_____

3. Which poem forms a shape to show what the poem is about?

_____

Plan Your Poem

Think of a subject for your poem. Choose one idea to write about.

My idea:

_____

- - - - - - - - - - - - - - - - - - -

_____

List words to tell about your subject. Write words that tell what your subject looks, sounds, smells, feels, or tastes like. List words to tell what you do with your subject. List words that tell how your subject acts. List words that tell how you feel about it.

My List

Draft Your Poem

Choose the kind of poem you will write. It can look like a poem on page 27. Will your poem rhyme? Will it follow a pattern? Will your poem be a shape? You decide!

Write a draft of your poem. Give your poem a title.

Title: _____

_____

_____

_____

_____

_____

_____

_____

_____

_____

_____

_____

More Help
Use words that have interesting sounds and meanings in your poem. Try to make your words say exactly what you mean.

Check Your Poem

Night Lights
~~Little Bugs~~   See how the title of this poem was changed.
∧

Change the word **dark** to a word that rhymes
with **bright**. Write the rhyming word above
this mark ∧ .

Firefly, firefly, shining so bright.

Firefly, firefly, light up the dark.
∧

Look at this poem. Use proofreaders's marks to correct
the misspelled words.

The cold wind blows

This way and that.

The wind took my sacrf

And then tok my hat.

Check your poem. Add rhyming words or change words
to more interesting ones. Then check your poem to make
sure all the words are spelled correctly.

Publish Your Poem

Is your poem just the way you want it? Write your final copy here. Don't forget to write a title.

Choose one way to share your poem.

• Fold a piece of colorful paper to make a card. Decorate the front. Write your poem inside. Then give it to a friend or family member.

• Do you have a tape recorder? Record yourself reading your poem. Then play the tape for others to hear.

What Is a Verb?

A **verb** is a word that tells about an action. Verbs tell what somebody is doing or what is happening.

Kangaroos hop. Lions stalk.
Snakes glide. People walk.

The words **hop**, **stalk**, **glide**, and **walk** are verbs

Write the verb in each sentence.

1. Five ducks waddle to the pond. _____

2. They jump in the cool water. _____

3. The ducks paddle with their feet. _____

4. They swim across to the other side. _____

Write the verb that best completes each sentence.

climb   run
hunt

5. Wild bears _____ for food in forests.

6. These animals _____ on the ground.

7. They can also _____ trees.

Verbs That Tell About Now

Some verbs tell about an action that happens now, or in the present. Add **s** to a verb that tells what one person, animal, or thing does.

One monkey **howls** out loud.
The other monkeys **howl** back.

Choose the correct verb to finish each sentence.

1. Noisy parrots _____ in the trees.
   sit   sits

2. The anteater _____ for insects to eat.
   look   looks

3. The sloth _____ upside down in trees.
   hang   hangs

4. Giant snakes _____ along the river bank.
   glide   glides

5. A fisherman bat _____ down to catch fish.
   swoop   swoops

6. A jaguar _____ through the jungle.
   prowl   prowls

7. The monkeys _____ for fruit in the trees.
   hunt   hunts

Verbs That Tell About the Past

Verbs can tell about an action that happened in the past. Many verbs add **ed** to tell about the past.

Lizards **live** today.
The verb **live** tells about the present.
Dinosaurs **lived** a long time ago.
The verb **lived** tells about the past.

Write a verb from the oval that tells about the present. Then find the past form of the verb and write it. One pair is done for you.

hunt   discovered
travel   worked
hunted   discover
work   traveled

Present | Past
1. hunt | hunted
2. ____ | ____
3. ____ | ____
4. ____ | ____

Complete each sentence by filling in a verb from the oval that tells about the past.

5. Last year scientists _____ to the desert.

6. They _____ for dinosaur fossils.

Verbs Is, Are, Was, and Were

The verbs **is** and **are** tell what things are like now.

That clown **is** silly.
Those clowns **are** silly.

The clowns are silly now.

The verbs **was** and **were** tell what things were like in the past.

That clown **was** sad.
Those clowns **were** sad.

The clowns were sad in the past.

Write **is**, **are**, **was**, or **were** to complete the sentences.

1. A backyard circus _____ fun.

2 My dog _____ barking now.

3. My sisters _____ happy to be clowns.

4. My parents _____ laughing and clapping.

5. Last year, my brother _____ scared of clowns.

6. The clowns _____ too loud for him back then.

Verbs Has, Have, and Had

The verbs **has** and **have** tell about action that is happening now. Use **has** with words that mean one person or thing.

Our community **has** a new school.

Use **have** with **I, you**, and words that name more than one person or thing.

I **have** a new class this year.

The verb **had** tells about the past.

Last year we **had** music class.

Complete the sentences with **has**, **have**, or **had**.

1. Our new school _____ a huge gym.

2. Last year, we _____ no gym.

3. We also _____ a great gym teacher now.

4. We _____ fun and learn a lot from him.

5. I wish we _____ gym twice a day!

6. Our class always _____ a great time.

Helping Verbs

The verbs **has**, **have**, and **had** can help main verbs show action. Use **has** with words that name one person or thing.

John **has** asked me to discuss sharks.

The verb **has** names one person. **Has** helps the main verb **asked** show action.

Use **have** with **I, you**, and words that name more than one person or thing.

I **have** told you about sharks before.

The verb **have** names **I. Have** helps the main verb **told** show action.

Complete the sentences with the helping verbs **has, have**, or **had**.

1. People _____ told stories about sharks for a long time.

2. Whale sharks _____ grown as long as 40 feet.

3. John _____ seen basking sharks and nurse sharks in the ocean.

4. But no sharks _____ ever hurt him.

5. No one _____ learned why sharks attack.

6. Once I _____ questioned a scientist about shark attacks.

Verbs Do, Go, and Come

The verbs **do**, **go**, and **come** tell about now. To tell what one person, animal, or thing does, add **es** to make **does** and **goes**. Add **s** to make **comes**.

When fall **comes** the geese go south for winter. They **do** this every year.

To tell about the past, **do** changes to **did**. **Go** changes to **went**, and **come** changes to **came**.

The geese **went** south last week.
They **did** a lot of flying.
The cold weather **came** early this year.

Underline the correct verb in each sentence.

1. Many people (go goes) south for winter, too.

2. They (do did) what the geese do.

3. When cold weather (come comes), they look for a warmer place to stay.

4. Last year many people (go went) to Florida.

5. Do you think these people (did does) a smart thing?

6. What would you (does do) if you had a chance to be warm all winter long?

7. Do you want to (come comes) with us to Florida?

Verbs Run, See, and Give

The verbs **run**, **see**, and **give** tell about now. To tell about the past, **run** changes to **ran**. **See** changes to **saw**, and **give** changes to **gave**.

Mom **runs** every day.
She **ran** twenty miles last week.

Underline the correct verb in each sentence.

1. I (see saw) mom race as often as I can.

2. Last year, I (see saw) mom race in Chicago.

3. Dad (gives gave) me a ticket to Chicago to meet her.

4. Hundreds of people (run ran) in the race.

5. Mom always (runs ran) fast.

6. I (see saw) her win third place.

7. The judges (give gave) her a medal.

8. I always (give gave) mom a hug when she wins.

Using Commas in Dates

Use a **comma** between the day and the year in a date.

A famous day in history is July 4, 1776.

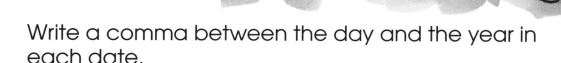

Write a comma between the day and the year in each date.

1. The Revolutionary War broke out on April 19   1775.

2. The Boston Tea Party was on December 16   1773.

3. The Civil War began on April 12   1861.

4. America went to war against Germany on April 6   1917.

5. Women got the right to vote on August 26   1920.

6. World War II began on September 1   1939.

7. Alan B. Shepard, Jr., became the first American in space on May 5   1961.

8. Write the date when you were born.

_____

_____

Using Commas in Addresses

Use a **comma** between the city and state in an address.

Waco, Texas
Deerfield, Illinois

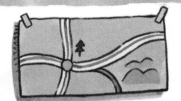

Write a comma between each city and state in the sentences.

1. The first public school opened in Boston   Massachusetts.

2. Laura Ingalls Wilder was born near Pepin   Wisconsin.

3. Disney World is in Orlando   Florida.

Write the city and state where you were born.

_____

4. _____

Fill in a comma between each city and state on the envelope. (CA is the abbreviation for California.)

Mr. I. M. Troll
12 Bridge St.
San Francisco CA 94107

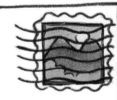

Mr. B. Goat Gruff
123 Green Hill Ave.
Menlo Park CA 94025

Using Commas in Series

Use **commas** between words in a series.
Your five senses are sight, hearing, touch, taste, and smell.

Write commas where they are needed in the sentences.

1. I like to see sunsets rainbows oceans and snow.

2. I like to hear music jokes and stories.

3. I like to touch kittens puppies grass and my pillow.

4. I like to taste oranges popcorn cocoa and pizza.

5. I like to smell roses the ocean and bread in the oven.

Use a complete sentence to answer this question.

6. What are your favorite games?

_____

- -

_____

Pronouns

A **pronoun** takes the place of a noun. **He, she, it, we, they,** and **I** are pronouns. **I** is always a capital.

Nouns	Pronouns
Cassie went to camp.	She went to camp.
The camp was this summer.	It was this summer.
The campers had fun.	They had fun.

Draw a line from the nouns to the pronouns that can take their place.

1. Cass and Kiyo   they
2. bunk bed   I
3. Mr. Thomas

_____ it

4. _____ he
      your name

Write pronouns to take the place of the nouns under the lines.

It   She
We   They

I saw a poster for summer camp. _____ said
               Mom and Dad

I could go. I told my friend about camp. _____
               Cass

wanted to go, too. _____ packed our suitcases.
    Cass and I

When we got to camp, we went to our cabin. _____
had bunk beds!   The cabin

Adjectives

An **adjective** tells more about a noun. Adjectives can describe number, size, or color.

There are **many** ladybugs flying outside.
How did these **tiny** insects get here?

Many adjectives come before the nouns they describe. Sometimes adjectives come after nouns.

The ladybugs are **colorful**.

Write the adjective that best completes each sentence.

Ladybugs are members of the beetle family.

This _____ lady is recognized by

red   big
black   little
many

her wings. Some ladybugs are _____ or orange

with black spots. Sometimes you will see a _____

ladybug with orange spots. The ladybug might have

a few or _____ spots on her wings. This tiny

insect helps people in a _____ way because

she eats other insects that kill crops.

What Adjectives Tell About

An **adjective** can tell how someone or something acts, sounds, feels, smells, or tastes.

The **hard** shell of a beetle protects it.
A cricket makes **loud** chirping sounds.
A grasshopper has **long** legs.

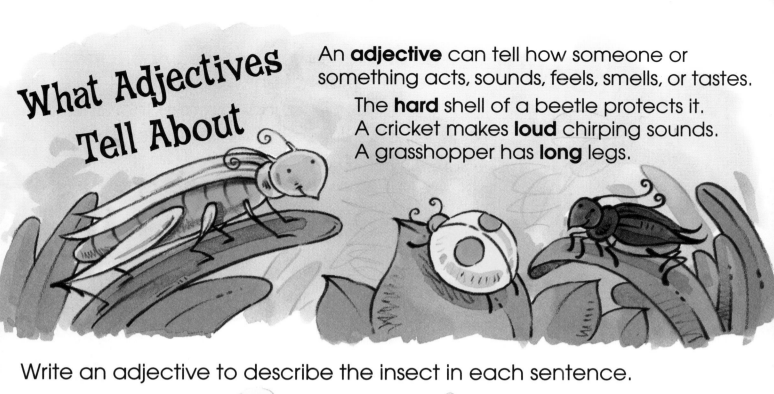

Write an adjective to describe the insect in each sentence.

snapping   beautiful   zigzag   fast   smelly   stubby

1. A butterfly is a _____ insect.

2. Caterpillars have _____ feet.

3. A beetle's click is a _____ sound.

4. The tiger beetle is a _____ runner.

5. The whirligig beetle makes _____ patterns when it swims.

6. The stink bug gives off a _____ odor if it is bothered.

Adjectives with er and est

Add **er** to an adjective to compare the differences between two nouns.

The North Star looks small**er** than the sun.

Add **est** to an adjective when comparing more than two nouns.

The sun is the bright**est** star of all.

Write the correct adjective to complete each sentence.

1. Mercury is the _____ planet to the sun.

    closer   closest

2. Mars is _____ than Earth.

    larger   largest

3. Saturn is _____ to Jupiter than Neptune.

    nearer   nearest

4. Pluto is the _____ distance from the sun.

    greater   greatest

5. It would take _____ to get to Jupiter

    longer   longest

from Earth than it would to get to Venus.

Adjectives: Comparative and Superlative Forms   ©1999 School Zone Publishing Company

What Is a Paragraph?

A **paragraph** is a group of sentences about one main idea. A paragraph begins with a **topic sentence** that tells the main idea. Indent the first sentence. **Detail sentences** tell about the main idea. A **closing sentence** ends the paragraph.

A Special Kind of Bird ◂------------- title

    The penguin is a very special bird. ◂------------- topic sentence
Penguins are birds, but they cannot fly. They can
dive, swim, and leap out of the water. The tiny
black and white feathers on a penguin keep it ◂------- detail sentences
warm. Penguins build a nest of stones instead of
twigs. When an egg is laid, the father penguin
keeps it warm. Penguins are not like other birds. ◂------- closing sentence

1. What does this paragraph tell about?
   Underline the answer.

   bird nests   robins   penguins

2. Draw a red line under the topic sentence.
3. Look at this idea web. Cross out details that do not tell
   about penguins. Cross out details that are not in the
   paragraph.

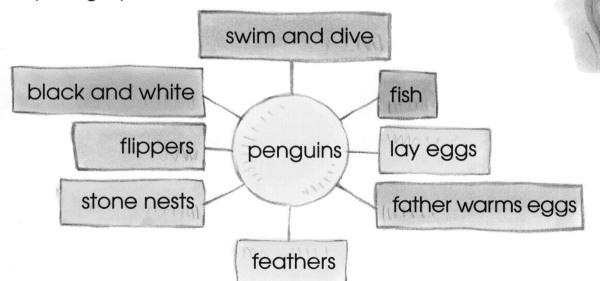

swim and dive

black and white   fish

flippers   penguins   lay eggs

stone nests   father warms eggs

feathers

Write a Describing Paragraph

A **describing paragraph** tells what a person, an animal, a place, or a thing is like. The writer uses describing words to help the reader see, hear, feel, taste, or smell.

In this describing paragraph, the writer tells what sea lions are like.

Sea Lions ← - title

    People like to watch sea lions. Many are found on the rocks along San Francisco's beach. Sea lions have sleek brown coats. They have little ears and flippers. Sea lions live on the land and in the water. They eat fish, squid, and shellfish. If you look for sea lions, listen for the loud barking. Sea lions are such fun to watch!

topic sentence

detail sentences

closing sentence

Circle the picture that shows the sea lion.

1. Draw a green line under words that describe what sea lions look like.
2. Draw a brown line under words that describe where sea lions live.
3. Draw a blue line under words that name what sea lions eat.

Plan Your Paragraph

You are ready to write your own describing paragraph
Pick a person, an animal, a place, or a thing to describe.

I will write a paragraph to describe

Make an idea web. Write your topic in the center circle.
In the boxes, write words that tell how your topic looks, sounds, feels, smells, or tastes.

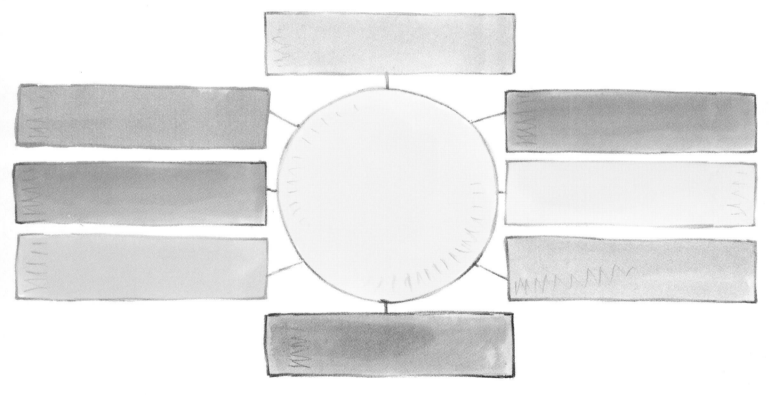

Show your idea web to someone. Talk about what you
plan to describe.

Do all your words describe your topic?   yes   no

Can you add more words?   yes   no

Draft Your Paragraph

Write your describing paragraph. Write a title for your
paragraph. Start with a topic sentence to tell your main
idea. Look at your idea web to write detail sentences.
End with a closing sentence.

More Help

Use plenty of describing words.
See pages 44-46 for ideas.

Check Your Paragraph

Describing words make writing more interesting. Use this mark ∧ to show where to add a word.

loud

If you look for sea lions, listen for the ∧barking.

Look at this mark ∧ in each sentence.
Above it add a describing word.

little   brown

1. Sea lions have sleek ∧coats.

2. They have ∧ears and flippers.

You can write longer sentences by
joining parts of two short ones.

Two sentences: Sea lions live on land.
              Sea lions live in the water.

Finish this longer sentence.

_____

3. Sea lions live on land and _____ .

Check your paragraph. See if you can join two short sentences to write
one longer sentence. Use this mark ∧ to show where you will add another
describing word.

Publish Your Paragraph

It's time to share your describing paragraph. First make a final copy of your writing.

_____

- -

_____

- -

_____

- -

_____

- -

_____

- -

_____

- -

_____

- -

Choose one way to share your paragraph.

- Read your paragraph to family members. Ask them to draw what you have described.
- Read your paragraph to a friend. Each time you come to the name of your topic, say, "blank" instead. When you have finished reading, ask your friend to guess who or what you described.

Antonyms

Antonyms are words whose meanings are opposite.
It is **easy** to see the Moon in the sky.
It is **hard** to see stars on a cloudy night.
The words **easy** and **hard** are antonyms.

Write the antonyms from each sentence.

The Big Dipper and Little Dipper
are two groups of stars.

1. _____

Open your eyes to find a
shooting star, and then close
them to make a wish.

2. _____

Some stars look dull, but the
North Star is very bright.

3. _____

Clear nights are the best time
to see stars and cloudy nights
are the worst time.

4. _____

5. _____

Synonyms

Synonyms are words whose meanings are the same or almost the same. Knowing synonyms helps you choose the right word when you write.

It is hard to **locate** some animals in the wild. You can't **find** them because of their colors.

The words **locate** and **find** are synonyms.

1. Find pairs of bugs with synonyms. Color each pair a different color.

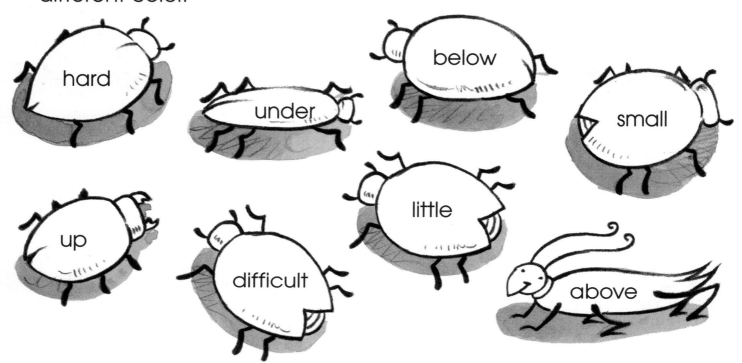

Write each sentence with a synonym for the underlined word.

2. It is <u>difficult</u> to spot a grasshopper in the grass.

_____

- -

_____

3. A walking stick is hiding <u>above</u> in the branches.

_____

- -

_____

4. Snails go <u>below</u> a clump of leaves to hide.

_____

- -

_____

Homophones

Homophones are words that sound the same but have different spellings and meanings.

The bear has a stubby **tail**.
Goldilocks and the Three Bears is a **tale**.

Tail and **tale** sound the same, but have different meanings. A tail is part of an animal's body, and a tale is a story.

Write the correct homophones to complete each sentence.

1. Our team _____ the game by _____ point.
   one   won   one   won

2. We _____ down a country _____.
   road   rode   road   rode

3. Let's go _____ the library at _____ o'clock.
   to   two   to   two

4. _____ you help me stack this _____?
   wood   would   wood   would

5. I _____ I'd get a _____ bike for my birthday.
   new   knew   new   knew

Contractions with Not

A **contraction** is a shorter word made from two longer words. An apostrophe (') shows where one or more letters have been left out.

In some contractions, the **o** in **not** is removed.

I **do not** think all animals belong in a zoo.
I **don't** think all animals belong in a zoo.

Draw lines from the words on the left to the contractions.

1. will not	isn't
2. is not	won't
3. can not	can't
4. are not	doesn't
5. does not	aren't

Write the contraction for the two words in each sentence.

6. Some animals _____ easy to keep in a zoo.
are not

7. A zoo _____ the best place for them to be.
is not

8. They _____ be happy unless they run free.
will not

Contractions with Will

Other **contractions** are made with **will**. An apostrophe (') takes the place of the letters **wi**.

I will learn about saving wildlife.
I'll learn about saving wildlife.

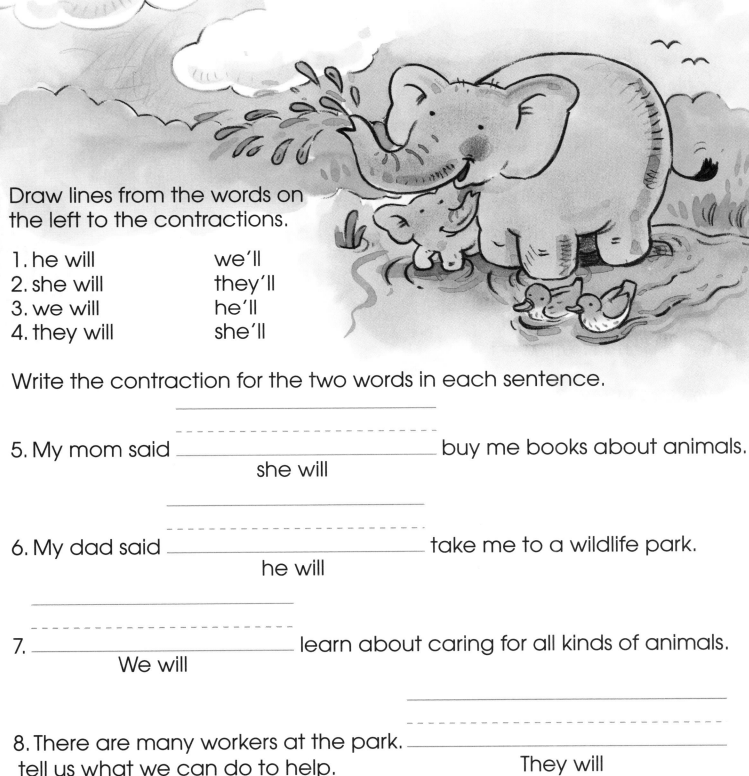

Draw lines from the words on the left to the contractions.

1. he will	we'll
2. she will	they'll
3. we will	he'll
4. they will	she'll

Write the contraction for the two words in each sentence.

5. My mom said ＿＿＿＿＿＿＿＿＿＿ buy me books about animals.
　　　　　　　　she will

6. My dad said ＿＿＿＿＿＿＿＿＿＿ take me to a wildlife park.
　　　　　　　he will

7. ＿＿＿＿＿＿＿＿＿＿ learn about caring for all kinds of animals.
　　We will

8. There are many workers at the park. ＿＿＿＿＿＿＿＿＿＿
tell us what we can do to help.　　　　　　They will

Dictionary: ABC Order

A **dictionary** lists words and their meanings. The words in a dictionary are in **ABC order**. This makes it easy to find the words you are looking for.

These words are in ABC order:

desert
earth
forest

a b c **d e f** g h i j k l m n o p q r s t u v w x y z

Are these words in ABC order? Circle **yes** or **no**.

1. mountain plain river   yes   no

2. hill valley river   yes   no

3. lake river ocean   yes   no

4. east north south west   yes   no

If words start with the same letter, look at the second letter to put them in ABC order. If the first two letters are the same, look at the third letter.

Write each group of words in ABC order to form a question. Circle **yes** or **no** to answer each question.

5. salt water are oceans   yes   no

6. are tall mountains   yes   no

7. deserts very wet are   yes   no

Dictionary: Guide Words

The **guide words** tell you the first and last entry words on a dictionary page.

If you are looking for the word **canyon**, you will find it on the page that has the guide words **camp** and **capital**. The letters **can** (<u>can</u>yon) come between the letters **cam** (<u>cam</u>p) and **cap** (<u>cap</u>ital) in ABC order.

Number these words **1**, **2**, **3** to show ABC order.

1. _____ ocean   _____ octopus   _____ oat

2. _____ forest   _____ football   _____ fog

3. _____ valley   _____ vase   _____ vegetable

Draw a line to match each word with the guide words that show where the word would be found in a dictionary.

Words	Guide Words
4. plain	dent—desk
5. mountain	iron—isn't
6. river	pizza—plant
7. desert	motor—mouse
8. island	ripe—road

Using a Dictionary

When you write, you may need to check the spelling or meaning of a word in a dictionary.

If you are writing about desert plants, you may want to find the word **cactus** in a dictionary. This is what one part of the dictionary page will look like.

guide words ----------▶ **cable car** ----------▶ **cactus**

entry word ----------▶ **ca′ble car**, a car drawn by an overhead cable.
definition ----------▶ It is used to carry people up and down a hill.

cac•tus (kak′təs), a plant that has a thick stem covered with spines instead of leaves.
example sentence ------▶ *Cactuses are found in desert areas of North and South America.*

plural forms ----------▶ *noun, plural* **cactuses** or **cacti**

picture ----------▶

Use the dictionary entries above. Write a sentence about cactus.

_____

_____

_____

Write a sentence about a cable car.

_____

_____

_____

Answers

Page 1

1. yes
2. no
3. yes
4. yes
5. no
6. We had a great day at the park.
7. We ate lunch under the trees.
8. All my friends were there.

Page 4

1. Jamal plays in the sand.
2. He likes to make sand castles.
3. He walks in the waves.
4. He finds seashells.
5. Some shells are white.
6. Sentences will vary.

Page 7

1. (.)
2. (!)
3. (.)
4. (.)
5. (.)
6. (!)
7. (!)
8. Exclamations will vary.

Page 10

The thing to be made or done should be described. Pictures should show steps.

Page 11

Directions will vary, but should include a title, order words, and various commands.

Page 12

<u>get</u> a plastic soda bottle, blue food coloring, and mineral oil⊙
~~What is your favorite soda?~~ First fill the bottle 3/4 full with water. ~~Water tastes good.~~ next add a few drops of blue food coloring⊙

Answers will vary.

Page 2

1. <u>Our family</u> visited Yellowstone Park. who
2. <u>The park</u> has lakes and springs. what
3. <u>People</u> camp in the park. who
4. <u>Stars</u> fill the night sky. what
5. <u>Forests</u> are everywhere. what
6. <u>Hikers</u> climb hills. who
7. Subjects will vary.
8. Subjects will vary.

Page 5

Check marks will vary.

1. Bananas are a good snack.
2. Cereal is a great breakfast food.
3. Oranges taste sweet.
4. Lettuce makes a fine salad.
5. Peas and carrots are yummy.
6. Statements will vary.

Page 8

1. Pass the ball.
2. Run fast.
3. Don't use your hands.
4. Keep your eye on the ball.
5. (.) statement
6. (?) question
7. (!) exclamation
8. (.) command

Page 13

Encourage your child to use one or both suggestions for sharing writing.

Page 14

1. My <u>uncle</u> has many <u>cows</u>.
2. See my <u>cousin</u> feed the <u>pigs</u>.
3. The <u>hens</u> and <u>chicks</u> are eating.
4. There is my <u>aunt</u> with her <u>horse</u>.

Page 3

1. Owls <u>hunt at night</u>.
2. Elk <u>eat green plants</u>.
3. Eagles <u>nest in the park</u>.
4. Water <u>shoots up from underground</u>.
5. Hikers <u>walk down trails</u>.
6. The forest <u>is quiet</u>.
7. Predicates will vary.
8. Predicates will vary.

Page 6

1. (?)
2. (.)
3. (.)
4. (?)
5. (?)
6. (?)
7. Questions will vary.
8. Statements will vary, but should answer questions.

Page 9

The directions tell how to make an ocean in a bottle.

You know what to do because the directions tell you what to do in order.

If you can't visit the ocean, you can make one in a bottle. <u>Get</u> a plastic soda bottle, blue food coloring, and mineral oil. <u>First fill</u> the bottle 3/4 full with water. <u>Next add</u> a few drops of blue food coloring. You can <u>add</u> some tiny plastic fish or shells if you want. <u>Then fill</u> the bottle with mineral oil. <u>Last, twist</u> the cap on tightly. <u>Hold</u> the bottle sideways. <u>Tip</u> it back and forth. <u>See</u> the ocean waves!

Page 15

The <u>family</u> is busy working on the <u>farm</u>. The <u>cows</u> are being milked. <u>Hens</u> are laying <u>eggs</u>. A <u>neighbor</u> is painting the <u>fence</u>. The <u>horse</u> waits in the <u>barn</u> to be brushed. My <u>uncle</u> is out in the <u>field</u> on his <u>tractor</u>.

People	Animals	Places	Things
family	cows	farm	eggs
neighbor	hens	barn	fence
uncle	horse	field	tractor

Sentences will vary but all nouns should be underlined.

Page 18

1. foxes; boxes
2. bunches; lunches
3. peaches; beaches
4. strawberries
5. pennies
6. stories

Page 21

1. Saturday Sat.
2. Pennsylvania PA
3. Avenue Ave.
4. March Mar.

Page 24

1. <u>Bird Watch</u>
2. <u>The Great Kapok Tree</u>
3. <u>If You Give a Pig a Pancake</u>
4. <u>Coyote Dreams</u>
5. <u>The Dinosaurs Came Back</u>

Page 27

1. "Rain" and the star poem
2. "My bird, Nicky"
3. the star poem

Page 16

1. an; a
2. an; a
3. a; an
4. an; a
5. a; an

Page 19

1. tooth teeth
2. foot feet
3. sheep sheep
4. goose geese
5. 10 children
6. 13 women
7. 19 sheep
8. 16 men

Page 22

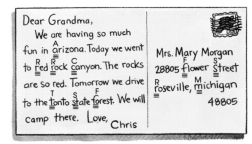

Addresses will vary.

Page 25

1. footprints
2. barefoot
3. sunglasses
4. seashells

barefoot
footprints
sunglasses
seashells

Page 28

Lists should include sense descriptions, actions, and feelings.

Page 29

Poem drafts should include titles.

Page 17

1. animals
2. cheetah
3. snakes
4. snails
5. horses
6. cat

Page 20

Pet Parade

The neighborhood is having a pet parade. aunt alice and tootsie are there. So is tom with ruff. Here come pat and matt with their cats, fluff and muff. There is wayne with his pig, petunia. See carmen's snake called slither. Last in line is grandpa jones. He calls his silly goat whiskers.

Sentences about pets will vary.

Page 23

1. Windmill Day
3. May
3. Saturday

I will spend july and august with my father. He lives in denver, colorado. On independence day we will visit the grand canyon. I will be away until labor day. That is the first monday in september.

Sentences about holidays will vary.

Page 26

1. a cold
2. a watch
3. a swing
4. a step

Page 30

Firefly, firefly, light up the ~~dark.~~ night.

The cold wind blows

This way and that.

The wind took my ~~saerf~~ scarf

And then ~~tok~~ took my hat.

Page 31

Poems will vary, but should show evidence of revision.

Page 34

1. hunt hunted
2. discover discovered
3. travel traveled
4. work worked
5. traveled
6. hunted

Page 35

1. is
2. is
3. are
4. are
5. was
6. were

Page 38

1. go
2. do
3. comes
4. went
5. did
6. do
7. come

Page 41

1. Boston, Massachusetts
2. Pepin, Wisconsin
3. Orlando, Florida
4. Cities and states will vary.

Page 44

little
red
black
many
big

Page 32

1. waddle
2. jump
3. paddle
4. swim
5. hunt
6. run
7. climb

Page 36

1. has
2. had
3. have
4. have
5. had
6. has

Page 39

1. see
2. saw
3. gave
4. ran
5. runs
6. saw
7. gave
8. give

Page 42

1. I like to see sunsets, rainbows, oceans, and snow.
2. I like to hear music, jokes, and stories.
3. I like to touch kittens, puppies, grass, and my pillow.
4. I like to taste oranges, popcorn, cocoa, and pizza.
5. I like to smell roses, the ocean, and bread in the oven.
6. Sentences will vary.

Page 45

1. beautiful
2. stubby
3. snapping
4. fast
5. zigzag
6. smelly

Page 33

1. sit
2. looks
3. hangs
4. glide
5. swoops
6. prowls
7. hunt

Page 37

1. have
2. have
3. has
4. have
5. has
6. had

Page 40

1. April 19, 1775
2. December 16, 1773
3. April 12, 1861
4. April 6, 1917
5. August 26, 1920
6. September 1, 1939
7. May 5, 1961
8. Dates will vary.

Page 43

1. Cass and Kiyo they
2. bunk bed it
3. Mr. Thomas he
4. Names will vary. I

They
She
We
It

Page 46

1. closest
2. larger
3. nearer
4. greatest
5. longer

Page 47

1. penguins
2. Topic sentence: The penguin is a very special bird.

3.

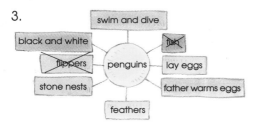

Page 51

1. Sea lions have sleek, ^brown^ coats.
2. They have ^little^ ears and flippers.

3. in the water

Help your child check his or her writing.

Page 54

Colors will vary, but synonyms should be the same color.

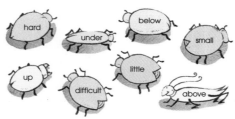

Answers will vary:

2. It is <u>hard</u> to spot a grasshopper in the grass.
3. A walking stick is hiding <u>up</u> in the branches.
4. Snails go <u>under</u> a clump of leaves to hide.

Page 59

1. 2   3   1
2. 3   2   1
3. 1   2   3
4. plain   pizza – plant
5. mountain   motor – mouse
6. river   ripe – road
7. desert   dent – desk
8. island   iron – isn't

Page 48

Sea Lions

People like to watch sea lions. Many are found <u>on the rocks along San Francisco's beach</u>. Sea lions have <u>sleek brown coats</u>. They have <u>little ears and flippers</u>. Sea lions live <u>on the land and in the water</u>. They eat <u>fish, squid, and shellfish</u>. If you look for sea lions, listen for the loud barking. Sea lions are such fun to watch!

Page 52

Completed paragraphs should show evidence of having been proofread and corrected.

Page 55

1. won   one
2. rode   road
3. to   two
4. Would   wood
5. knew   new

Page 57

1. he will   he'll
2. she will   she'll
3. we will   we'll
4. they will   they'll
5. she'll
6. he'll
7. We'll
8. They'll

Page 60

Sentences will vary, but the words **cactus** and **cable car** should be used correctly.

Page 49

Topics of describing paragraphs and idea webs will vary.

Page 50

Describing paragraphs should include titles, topic sentences, detail sentences, and closing sentences.

Page 53

1. Big   2. Open
   Little   close

3. dull   4. Clear
   bright   cloudy

5. best
   worst

Page 56

1. will not   won't
2. is not   isn't
3. can not   can't
4. are not   aren't
5. does not   doesn't
6. aren't
7. isn't
8. won't

Page 58

1. yes
2. no
3. no
4. yes
5. Are oceans salt water?   yes
6. Are mountains tall?   yes
7. Are deserts very wet?   no